Testing the Drink

Kevin Connelly

PublishAmerica
Baltimore

© 2004 by Kevin Connelly.

All rights reserved. No part of this book may be reproduced, stored in a retrieval system or transmitted in any form or by any means without the prior written permission of the publishers, except by a reviewer who may quote brief passages in a review to be printed in a newspaper, magazine or journal.

First printing

ISBN: 1-4137-2522-8
PUBLISHED BY PUBLISHAMERICA, LLLP
www.publishamerica.com
Baltimore

Printed in the United States of America

This book is dedicated to Jason Balalaos.

I would like to thank Philippe Roberts-Haas for providing the illustration for the cover. He has beautifully depicted a scene from my work's titular piece. I wish him future success in his craft.

Harrow Hell

These horrors are due, the barrier's broke;
my friends, can't you hear, the harriers come?
The hares are all sheared; how scary they croak!
We've dyed all their thumbs the hue of a bum!
I've cried: "Harrow hell, and try for the toads,
you'll find on the road, the edges are gums,
rum soaked, it's teething, attempting to goad
the end; recant fear, and enter the tun!"
The tummy's rotund, but narrows as soon
as you pass its lips; jazz on a bassoon.
The mouth of a bass can babble a boon:
"The heart on my sleeve is from a baboon!"
Now, out of this sieve, it's time to attune;
for doubting my class can tackle a tune!

Funeral Arrangements

No, I shouldn't cry, I might miss her move,
embalmed with rigor; swearing by flickers:
"Mom, I wouldn't lie," tonight by the moon,
I'm calm and composed, my will, with a rose,
placed on your shell, two shillings on your face,
I'm not killing grace, I'm planting mistakes!
"Alarmingly grave! This can't be my fate!"
What did you expect, a place for respect?
"I request a vase!" The flowers won't keep;
sequestered above, my mantle of love.
"My marrow is chilled; your prowess is key!"
The powers that be allow her to speak!
"Too narrow for child, your seed will sour!"
My sorrow is mild; I'll beat this shower.

Spinning Chamber

Bashful pansophist, a tad Basho-esque;
a tadpole kisses the princess's basque,
in the King's English, since you have to ask;
is it an issue for you if I bask?
"If it's a bisque you want, a bisque you'll get;
the soup or the bowl, tennis or croquet?
Red-yellow skin is the risk you accept;
I've tested the drink, my whistle is wet!"
Bedfellows akin, let the truth be told,
if God is the tree, the thistle is Set;
how hard can it be to speak tête-à-tête?
Yet, who's in control, when his soul is sold?
Roulette in Seoul, going tit for tat;
a pistol clicks on either this or that!

Off with Her Head

I precess a top, a precipice reached;
I stand by the lip, proceeding to pot,
the Medusa's strands; these precieuses preached:
"A tip: It'll peak; the Recent will rot!
You'll free us from flesh!" But recess is out;
the pecks from your beaks rip Jesus' brow!
"We vow once we're tapped, we'll mortar this mount;
even Olympus!" You say Zeus's house!?
"We're saying, we'll seine, to stay in Sane's wake;
a seiche: as a sash on a lady's waist;
slash, a scythe to crops; a rock to Cyclops…"
IROCs to Wops, sike, I stick by my blocks,
like street signs and lights, this pastiche lasted;
I watch as these locks leave a canvas plastered!

Song of the Myope

"A caroling babe?" Bah! I abhor all!
Lambs are iambic; they baa a choral!
"I'll corral the bulls; a toreador…"
I've think we've all heard that story before!
"A sparrow with sage in it's maw to awe?"
That bothersome hawk? In the morn it caws!
"I think you're confused, it's barely a tuft!"
But they both have beaks; a chirp is enough!
My quota is reached, for passion to burn;
infatuation's ash got tapped in urns!
I drink to delude my work on this Earth;
so give me your birds and your babes at birth!
"Why you worthless fu…" a cuss is a curse;
and cause to abruptly finish this verse.

The Reaper

I write of an Irish blind scytheman,
who dashed with the speed of a hyphen;
a child fell asleep,
in the field he reaped-
and now she's minus a hymen!

Dirty Pool

A cue's a rabbit, hold it askew to
muse its habitat, as you scope it's gait;
so cute and rapid, it's turning puce-blue;
an acute defense. Wind opens the gate,
the pickets are mute; it fell for the bait!
A mouse in a pussy's mouth is pâté!
Remember to stay, each month on this day,
away from the table, patting your pate;
batting your lashes, you'll just have to wait,
and learn what few do; chalk it up to date.
A friend of a friend, knew a duce who,
used this habit as a way to make dew.
There's no hope in faith; a pause is passé.
Rather then muss hares, I pass by masse.

Shaking Hands

I burr, in the cold, it concurs with churrs;
the bugs are so bold, they're building my bier!
Or is it a plank; but where is the pier?
Oh, dear! They're flanking! Beware of your peers!
Know fear and thank it for being a cur;
showing you liars, they're buying you beers!
Raising their flutes up, and crying out cheers!
The lyres appear; each note is a bur,
attached to your fur, no matter how mere:
a raisin; a mar, the size of a blur;
the bobber; the hook, attempting to lure;
a purr is a sigh, suggesting a leer.
I'm sure it's a sign; when it rains, it pours!
The robber! The crook! Redemption is pure!

Sea Arms

The way that I walk depends on the elms:
"One hull of a plank!" I'm off the deep end;
Talk hullabaloo, half-asleep, tanked and
senseless; my sea arms, numb as duns get alms.
Come and get some cents; crumbs run to get on:
"I say that he talks!" "I swear that he ohms!"
Home alone I honed this, no disrespect
to Tibetan kids, but that's all off dome.
Words are citizens; I just check the census.
When a word is born, I check dependents;
then check the rhyme like Tip and the Questers.
Intellects a wick; you lit the scented!
I sense dissension, then script this sentence:
You're a paragraph! Go get indented!

Grilling

A human is slued; control is a myth.
"But if I am glued what's with a mass missed?
Something is amidst within this mish-mash;
humid and dewy, my soul is the mist!"
A goal is just math; a gist, I suggest.
"But I can't accept this ageist gift!
I feel I am due some Aegean depth;
aboard this raft you've deftly set adrift."
Yes, your correct in requesting a gaff…
"To catch a fish with!? Your answers a laugh!
I'd rather a net, to collect the daft;
they leapt, I gathered: *Can you gauge it yet?*"
There's only days left; my intents a craft.
Making you tense up- I invent aghast!

Paper Faith

In lieu of the leis, placed over the heads,
of vacationing Ted's, Louis' and Ché's:
a noose's sun ray; sways over the chaise,
dangling dusk in the form of the dead.
Aloof in the haze, confusing the bees,
spilling his seed, in his formative days,
a pang of mistrust while willing this deed,
the hue of his face was normally green.
A deist who strays, is planning to praise;
there's truth in this lie: to pray is to plea.
Chiasmus mirrored in pans used to braise,
beef from the killing, a fleur-de-lis phrase:
"Your teeth for my tooth; a tusk for a fang.
A trumpet to blow! A musket to bang!"

Presenting Columbus

I got my sea legs, consigliore!
My lore of the shore, you'll adore, I'm sure!
"Sir, can you discern, when it's your turn or,
have you gone the way of ale and turnips!?
So Gael of the sea, regale us, you saw?
Guffaws will ensue as soon as you yawn!
Sinews are winnows; they crack up our yaw,
like painted windows, by fates, they are sewn."
Six hands are pawing; Pilate is the pawn,
by dawn, he'll mourn and bring sins to the pew,
and since we are due, then hence we are born!
Phew! I narrowly evaded their scorn!
An arrow harpoons, cartooning a prawn:
His plan is to prune! He's darting through yews!

Killie Traps

These fish can swim in, but they can't swim out.
This water will win, without any doubt,
Hawkins suggested a nominal point:
"Death by Gravity will surely anoint!"
Glued to their chair arms, the surly will pout:
"Ethereal bowties abominate joints;
even on cherubs turned girly with gout,
gabbing their vowels and grabbing their groins,
like charms below chins," a lisp in their jowls,
"Allow me a kiss!" in the raspiest voice,
rubbing the finish and clasping the dowel;
while asking out loud, there's hardly a choice:
Who's behind flounders? I whisper to owls;
Imploding funnels dispense within bowels!

Starboard Side

I harbor *Regret*, for what I have done,
is dock my ship; did you expect a sin?
What the hell's that noise?! Where the heck's a din?!
My sextant is poised inspecting the sun.
The arbor is wet, the cork is a sponge;
the eldest line snaps, by pumice- expunged!
A sextet at twelve has only begun,
to offer belles rings and leave the strings strummed.
The barber will snip, a quarter to one,
giving time a trim's dependent on wind;
while stepping inside a bent hexagon,
albeit chalk traced, there's a hex on him!
You'll seldom find fit, punishment to come;
we'll meet at your place, and sit next to kin!

Just For Kicks

The sole of a brogue's like dragging a drogue,
funneling mud as grubs tunnel in droves;
so lo and behold, he's holding a grudge:
This cap wears a patch, he dabbles in drugs;
wobbles a bit and smells fennel in groves;
loathes with a switch like a kennel of dogs;
coddles a witch to spell trouble for love.
She doubles the breeze and brushes the logs;
cuts through the fog and continues to rove,
comes to your home and gives life to your loaves:
"Oh! The taste is…goodness gracious…odes!"
Tomes are wasted though; vague notions in vogue!
Oh him? He's a ham! His hymn is an ohm;
he hums it within: a tomb for a rogue!

A Trip to Limerick

There once was a dude named Ulysses,
who traveled by sea to the cities;
he planned to come home,
but those Sirens moaned:
"Please, stay between two sets of titties!"

Minerva Heard

A halcyon flaps: its span is a fleet;
to measure by feet's a fluke upon flake.
A womb of azure can capture a lake;
a cloud is a room, accruing a leak,
as sure as I am this rapture is late;
it's been at least a week after the date,
a halogen lamp was lit in your place,
it's all in good faith; perhaps if we wait,
we won't need to weep, and treasure keepsakes;
I'm ruining the wake! An answer escapes:
"This man must lack sleep, aboard his hackney;
the moon is his horse, drawing the neap up.
A loon plots it's course, boring and hackneyed;
according to suns, dawning, he needs love!"

*An aside to me, the tide's the sea's breath,
and beside the beach, the nape of my neck,
I see an egret, and reference regret;
My pride- its wet beak, prying as I set.*

Testing The Drink

I fish with a pole, hook, line and sinkers;
thinking of dinner, because I have none:
"A loan with my Id? Pockets turn sphincters!
Nine pieces of squid will get this job done!"

Ogling the locks, or wisps of a Wasp,
stolidly I clock each flip, flap and flop;
atop the coppery skin of the sea,
feet prop the sop, to dock 'n sup in peace.

Shooing the settled, I nettle the goop;
oodles of bait fish swoop to regroup it:
"Detritus minded! Iridescent coup!
Huddle, but the mud'll make it stupid!"

Composing my mind, I retract that line;
bumbling with bob, and twiddling twine:
"Your fish did fine, gobblin' clumps in lanes;
from the choppy wake, to the dumps of twains!"

I change my station, when the depth is one,
to praise the mirror of Our Deadly Sun:
"Gone back to lumping? I'm your chump and chum!
This murk is mad ill! When it gloms, it's glum!"

In slumber I shake, R.E.M. raped by red rum;
underneath my bed, I hear a tape hum!
Numbers and rubbish of future blunders:
"Remember your teeth! Sutured in blubber!"

Humming madrigals, nothing matters still;
the male Emily, noting raps on sills!
Doting by the rill, a crab is combing;
mail me my Emmy! The gale is coming!

A Gael at galas; a glass or chalice?
Half empty or full? Of bull or malice?
Just tempt me, and I'll blow the gaff in spite!
Trusting the penny! Doing ads for Sprite!

I'm whittling wood, beginning to fin;
a fan is a friend, who thinks this is good?
My hood can't begin to sip more then gin!
Understood, I test what The Gods call food.

The Pomp from Old Dough may dabble in sails,
but my Pop used to go: "Snails beget salt!
They're wet in their pink, so they'll always fail;
when testing our drink, they flail at its fault!

Men of the Bulkhead, our job's to get crisp;
greasing our motors like Greeks did with piss!
Catch in our fists, we sulk, reddened to pipe:
'This one's for Mother, not Jesus H. Christ!'

Prismatic oil's like scaling a cod,
or jogging a schist, resisting the Bog.
This scalpel of God gives the bod stitches:
'All the cogs wish for shish-ka-bob dishes!'

Sourly we jib, chew our cud and gripe:
'Cripes! We lug the crates; they grip jugs and crepes?!'
Hourly they sit, chug their grapes and spew:
'Tripe! Your sow worthy faces gape askew!

'Asthmatic toilers, stop jibing and jig!
I'm boiling a pig; start bribing your judge!'
Resembling Frank, but Porky won't budge;
a recoiling sprig, I trembled so big!

'A bib for jabbed ribs!,' I stagger on stage;
a swagger from sage, I blather irate:
'I spit at your age, no rigor, I rage!
I will die later! Patched in as Pi rates!'

As I aspirate, my eyes dilate death,
'Yes...a pirates death!,' My breath is thinning;
yet, as I play wreaths, it all starts to mesh:
There's more to destiny than bread winning!"

A dollar a fib, for the glib scholars!
Fobbing on my watch? Your collar is bleached!
"The color was deep!," now your gob hollers,
"grubbing for clovers, your cover is breached!"

The kitschiest snobs, sob on and pip up:
"Off cobs in Sodom, you got bombed with cads!"
To soften my nib, I spoke to the Hub:
"Hobbled, as I nag and bitch for this pap..."

The din of these duns is dimming me some;
I've been the dunce once, stumbling fundless.
I hid in coffins, pining, dumb and stressed;
and since this stunt I've been drumming up sums!

"Tom is a big Whig! His thumb is his tomb!
He hums out of tune while wagging his tomes!"
To brag this gig is to atone for Rome;
I'm gagged in my home, roaming in one room!

Where's my galoshes? Where are my marshes?
Fried amidst a white Diet of starches,
I march to the heart, departing to mop;
their flimflam is fop! "Hold up! Hold up! Stop!"

The docks, where I weep, as I filet carp,
"I used to play harp, now I just play parts!"
A piece is a whole, though, so I'll stay strung;
by bow and by lung, [cough] till my day's come!

I sit in my skiff, my cloud and my skin;
no books allowed! They're too stiff to follow!
I'm your sallow crook, beginning to skim;
brimming so loud, to make this brook fallow!

Every bridge has gnomes, rigging to rub you's!
[Zigzagging digits!] You dig Mister Zinn?!
"Who's cloning my phone? It flickers like Zeus!"
Knickers for niggards! Bigots yap with yin!

The prop is my dog; her mussels are ticks.
No collar will fit; she must shake her shit!
Tussling with leash, I'm choking my lass;
as it kicks over, I fall on my ass!

Her muscles have tics, but she's brollicky;
a rollicking bitch, butt's all colicky,
frolics in rotten beef and broccolis;
got a lease on life; mortgaged cottage cheese!

Neither hear or tear, breathing ether's heirs,
here in the nether, blithe hares breed on tiers;
it's tight as a tithe, to lathe air like tin,
as lichens unite, and lay there so lithe!

Nearest to the rear, I'm raring to moor;
right ear in the mire, where it's clear I'm mere!
This era of 'mares is pairing the poor:
"You spark this pyre and he'll wear the mar!"

The tar is torn between spleen and the shin;
Shall he melt with all, or collect pelts ale'd?
"The latter is self, but aren't we shale?"
No doubt, the law barred this bard for this sin!

A jar of Thorazine will glean my glen,
if a pen can lamp or lean like at Lent;
by the advent, I seem aloof for goose,
or a hoof to beef; my laws are too loose!

I hook to a beat; a raw cockle roosts,
meant for a cloister, he's preying to rend!
"Mending an oyster is like paying rent:
I look to defeat, and coddle a ruse!"

Shining for a dime, I cobbled a boot;
"Now I'm making cents! I'll waddle out brine!
Canadian geese is what I'm about;
defense is aiding a wattle to bind!"

Out of the blue shirt, I vow to rue this:
"My poop for the Pope! Duty is priesthood!
My view is due east, so the bow's Buddhist;
Why stoop with a slope when the yeast is good?

I'm on my last leg, it's hard to keep up;"
we'll buy you a peg... "or food to heat up?
Unleavened, but no, no feast for the gimp;
this Easter, I egg; ebbing but not limp!"

The hounds have found me, with bounded bounty,
they heard of my folks in Nassau County!
Zounds! That sound you make when your astounded;
clouds! Surrounded as you bake an ounce down.

This seer is a heel! He swears by our hall!
He's hailing the kale; "and halving your bell!"
His hull is a hill! He sears in our hell!
The career of a seal; "having a ball!"

In a whale's belly I wail by the wall,
feeling like veal as I steer from the helm:
"Its spine is a keel the size of an elm;
a rind like an eel's, I'll thrive off the salt!

"Remind me I'm real," I mumble to me,
"Is this a Mitzvah? 'How humble is he?'"
I crumble like peat in the mitts of man;
dropping the seed in and mixing the sand,

dripping the mist on and heating the pit;
sprouting this season, leaving a thistle!
Doubting my reason? Heed this epistle:
I grease the pistons by bleeding my fist!

I bumble like bees, itching for a hive:
"I'll greet their treason, hidden in a hide;
grumbling for treats, driven by this dive,
wishing death on those that wish that I'd died!

Ere I direly dare to err like deer,
either I'll endure or herd with my Herr!"
This ire's pear shaped; I'm hurt with no hair!
"Never was a tare mistaken for Dear!"

A straggler laughs, released from his tact;
He reads from my tract and muses a tack!
"A gag from the pack, abuses the pact;
 I see how his gab confuses the past!

"Were he to lead curs to the shore with flair,
leapers would worry, to the fore, I'm sure!
Wood for his Libras, are spared, two by four;"
Troubadours see stars! Pay their fare and stare!

"Adore these steel bars, so he won't steal cars;"
they plead with Shakers, "Grenades leave vapors!
This spade kneads acres!" these racists deal cards,
"Abhor those real bards, displayed in cases!"

No peers up to par, are nearby my pier;
paring a lira, the bar is my pew:
"At least a gabble will earn a few leers!
I'll rabble rouse fears to fill urns and flues!"

The phial is full; a pull defiles!
A pile of pearls spilt girlishly while,
Miltonian wiles churlishly spur the,
etudes to toast flutes and wilt fleur-de-lis!

The filers a fern, potted and plastic,
God damns and darns him, I say it's curtains!
"What the hell is heck?" He says: "It pertains
to rancor we learned in all those classics."

Terming an anchor, my liquid asset,
the lanterns are gassed; I blew a gasket!
A tern is fastened, I caw as a cue;
I can't break the ice! I thought it acute!

I thaw; I taw you, my puddy, I did!
I did! It dawned on, though sooty as Sid,
carving his chest up, *Nancy* it said;
it's sad, they used him, and left him for dead.

Sense for the greedy? Try lint for you all!
Poseidon gave steeds, I make the sea scald!
A maitre d' serves what the chef cooks up;
stirred with a trident, words you should look up!

Quintessential rules to live by and win:
Reside in the reeds and squint at the sun;
rely on your deeds, and think that you've won;
splint a broken arm, the wound is a sin!

The paw of a bear, bared far from its lair,
and as the lore goes, appearing to lure;
ask the Lord dosing, "Is he fierce, not fair?
Please take care to show how his fur is cured!"

Desire, my Sir, or Madam, perhaps,
was said, by madmen, to turn back in laps,
along the channel, a gong's haiku claps;
its rhapsody lapses to buy you daps!

A miserly chap, or bagman, perhaps,
was dead for a week as the bayou sapped,
that essence of self that holds us all back:
Your body's a corpse; of course you knew that!

Without, trapped within, even my kin doubts;
a moth flutters love, crazed in our King's mouth!?
Sad, but truly yours, I sign *Kevin C.*;
I sigh heavy...and resign heavenly:

"Life's a bitch, I left her in the nineties;
jumped in Sergio, met her kick shopping,
clacking on spearmint, her ego: mighty;
built like pyramids, better pick cotton!"

Is this rogue Judas? Brutus to Popeye?
Spinach in Greenwich, with fruit flies who spy?
Nietzsche in Enyce, blush Nikes like rouge;
found my niche in niceties, plus rude boos!

"Lauren!" I yearn for the dew on a bur;
when I mourn, her mane replaces my slurs!
Nay! a drawn out yawn, or this yarn I burp:
"Dame in a straw boat, you were born by surfs!"

My catfish will purr: "My kiss is not poor!
Just look in my purse; I smacked my own lips
and laid off the nurse! Get paid off your verse;
I'll spay our impure!" That bitch had the nerve!

I furrow my brow, earnestly twitching
in Oedipal rage, a man is a nun?!
Incredible change! My wrists need switching;
"My habit needs kicking! Amen! I'll come!"

I fell to the floor, pouring libations:
"Pray at the first stair before you step up;
throwing tomatoes, trying to catch up!
Whores get wet up devouring my sons!"

To conjure her face, reminds me of Death;
the angle, the grace that binds me to faith!
The collar I don, the color of wraiths,
or angels; I taste...no wait! Why waste breath?!

Gungadin, you made a fatal mistake;
you fed Ganesh peanuts! He's no dumbo!
Bathe in dung for me and speak yo' mumbo;
my heart of darkness palpitates distaste!

I must have Miss Took, like Paris in heat;
I ravaged your wrists, you bandaged my feet!
Head in an oven, excuse...bread rather;"
her coven of hens accuse my chatter,

of being "woven," humph! I dread thimbles!
Clove hitch to a spar! Doves are my gimbals!
Do you bitch at stoves?! No! See, yet you cook!
Now you get the book: (thump!) "My head tickles...

"Carry-on Bally! Valet at ballets!"
Tarry in valleys!? Carrion dally!?
"Israeli chalets! Married in Bali!"
Carry on Sally! I rarely tally!

Her veil sways rally my prawn like baleen:
"Let me play the rake! Your lawn will stay green!"
Skirting these issues, curtailed in a bun,
this pawn can't take queens, only awake one.

My crush on a guppy ended up stream,
plump from the anguish, she blushed angrily:
"Pollute then praise me? Am I the Ganges?
In between the Twain, tamed only to teem!?

I want to wane too!" But you whine too much!
"I want to dine now." The refined go Dutch;
cows go to Pasteur! Where is the laughter?!
"Too much wine I guess...where is the pastor?"

I axe the question, without a hatchet;
you die to say "yes!" batting your lashes!
I belt out like Pops: "Buckle down hatches!
Babies to cradles; ashes to ashes!"

Chuckles drown sadness, up to the rafters;
a bat sings Hamlet, crashing through racket:
"To see or not to? Without attachments?
My uncle the wop lived by the ratchet!

"I, lag on the lam, do solemnly swear,
cuss, curse, dis and snap like Golem, beware!
Thus, this thirst is first and foremost to toast,
with a hiss, this husk which is host to ghosts!'"

My throat just won't close, thrust a note to tisk,
those who risk their nose to expose my niche:
"Who dares to salaam as they gag on ham?
Adam are you there? I thought so, I Am!"

Lunging for latches: a knuckle to joint,
my number two point will binge to hinge gaits!
Rescinding my faith, in slumber we're joined;
by rashes in groins: the fringe of a jape!

I cringe at the shape of a twin conjoined;
the skin on an ape; a two-sided coin!
A wrinkle unnerves; a freckle is Death;
a sickle unearths a fickler Seth!

A stickler sent to sticker cassettes,
hinders what's def to discredit the left:
"If your chins not cleft, check it at exits!
Existentialist- regret to exist!"

Scented envelopes, letters never sent;
hesitant, second guessing sentiments.
Tension collects like sediments in cliffs;
pent up, regression is my repentance!

What's frail as a flea, yet sized for a tent?
A clown's rubber nose is read with dissent;
I'll down one of those, the red with the scent!
My plea is so pale, yet ripe with intent!

I guzzle the blood of Jesus H. Christ,
throw rice on a tryst, and worship it thrice!
"How nicely they sing," a guinea pig thirsts;
we nuzzle this thing!? Our fetus is cursed!

A gaggle of geese Bernoulli a Beat;
edges get pestled and gargle on peat:
"Gabling ripples! Correction of Pete's!
Now, your lips are the complexion of beets!"

Erecting a mast, "At last you are wooed!
I'll strangle these sheep if they can't be shooed!"
Ejected from mass, I asked if we should;
you cried and said: "Yes. On a raft of wood;

people drift apart," you whisper to wind,
"A blunder a day is wasting a waltz!"
I wonder away: "Can she taste the salt?"
If evil's an art, my whiskers are singed!

My easels an ark, the skippers will swab
the Devil out decks, to leave not a mark!
"We double in debt," they whimper to God,
"We read lots of Mark! Why lead us to dark?"

Heaving up kippers, they'll eat not with sharks,
believing in Marx, their sister would flip:
"I need a shoe horn, this slipper won't fit!"
There's trouble in bed; I'll sleep off this farce!

I'm taking a dip! The stone is taught,
imagine it's brick in cold New York;
your mind is callused, so is a toe,
I'm so off the road, like Alice through holes.

I paint a portrait. "Someone is missing;
where is your Father!?" He went out fishing.
"A table for twelve?" invents a miser,
"Sable and selfish!" Fodder for Pfizer!

You think God is dead? I think He's a lie;
I watched Peter write, and seen his eye wink!
I've tested his drink, my spleen is not pink!
There's life in this drink, so drink till you die!"

Oozing Midori, like a twist to lime,
lame end gurgling, my petals taste thyme:
"Taming burgles time, taken by metals;
meddling loses its pace in kettles."

On course with mettle! Gun it for Kelly!
Gelling in pithy, my fifty-horse neighs;
a helping of kelp wrenches his belly,
my knave dispenses his cycles in waves!

Once again: Chaos! Revealing your dawn;
drawn to this Pesach, the killies are fauns.
Unraveled with leagues, they flop as they drown;
gaveling flippers, and gills that flap frowns!

Swans reveled in form, a feat that felt Luke;
escaping to lakes, all named "Drake," they leak.
My namesake rests in a floor of felled fluke;
ingesting my puke, while skating in fleets!

Requesting this dude sequestered in suds,
like, "Noah, you ever, ever heard of?"
Geppetto the wet? Some say he's the sods;
or trapped in a whale, delaying the odds.

Proteus! The krill, gummed by a rorqual?!
No jute to floss with, Pro' found his lost wit:
"A toothless portal? Its goatee is moss!
This kill won't quell roars; I'll snorkel in Morse!"

The gulls with dull bills, will mill in my dale,
mull over dill bales and till it to nil;
all gall and no bull, I'll stay gullible:
"I'm bawling for Baal! Tell my gal I'm nailed!"

Play Christ in polo, his horse trots on pools;
post-game he'll school you: "Discourse plots on fools!
So, lo and behold, though nice you may drool;
to talk is a tool." He taught me his rule.

I'm off to the duel; too often to tell,
have I lost or won? Tone deaf to the Belle!
Too hefty to lift, a bull in China,
deftly is felled; pleasant reminders!

Your soul is a chime, a bell, a cymbal;
controlling a rhyme, but bah! A symbol?!
An organ we reach with digits in time,
will wither in lime, while digging for thyme!

I stall like latrines, cake in the middle;
your in my tureen, a lake of urine,
my impression of the shroud of Turin,
cloud nine for turbans slaked by a missal!

Nobly I fall, and Nobody showed,
Cyclopic foresight in a cave of sheep:
"Dog, I'm Pavlov's bitch! I behave to bleeps!
Blinded, as they clopped away on a boat!"

Notably, I recall, they left me so wowed;
without a sunglass, or a salve to heal!
My laughs like a squeal, and oh how I howled:
"This calve I'm eating made Achilles weep:

"Laid me still in sleep, the way that he mooed;
paid me lip service, but the points were moot!'"
While preying on muted colors I gloat:
I can goad a god by slaying a goat!

I'm taking a dip; a dab hand's a fin!
This is tit-for-tat; a dad tans a man!
Akin to Lincoln? Little violins!
Small tarantellas; she's raising a fan.

I'm calling dibs on, what riffs a Gibson,
the fist the rings on, what's rife with glib dung?
The flash you sing for, I slash the string on,
this Axl prose is cause to sling guns.

Holy Mackerel! I bait, you tackle;
so see, a hack'll spackle for his caste!
Checked kings can't castle; you wait to cackle:
"A hackle is split! Shackled for a cask!"

I bade you farewell, feral as a pit;
leashed up it lashes, attached to your junk.
Relish my pickle, in spanglish you jib:
"Si, anos aqui!" You leak out the punch!

"I hunt pianos for eighty-eight keys,"
an elephants grave whispers me thunder;
a tundra shivers: "Me timbers to meet
your day to day needs leave me in hunger!"

I beat out your hunch, you're Richard the Third;
fuck you and your horse, just glue for my bind!
you dick with the herds, for thee and for thine,
a tee-time for nine?! I flip you the bird!

At a loss for words, I work at the mart;
more snarky then smart, I'm serving the parched.
I cross their *T's* and dot their ides of March,
I force their treason, plotting my pride's part:

"It will titillate; sit still! We'll be late!
This is delicate: the finest linen,
the spiders are weaving! I'll leave today!
My design is sin! It smells of tin, men!"

Expatriot

If stress is a test, I'm in detention, getting demerits, suspended, wedged with the rest of the derelicts with Tourette's (Dyslexics with recessive genetics, regularly neglected since bassinets, rejected mental wrecks headed directly to cigarettes; stems; amphetamines; ecstasy; heroin; ketamine; sedatives; Excedrin; whatever, I mean, etcetera.); getting lectured, yet again, for etching negative sentiments on my desk. Attention deficit, Eddie Vedder-esque in a sweater, yes, with less discretion then retching mescaline heads guessing questions and betting like Tribeck's guests- sweating. Never hesitant, to express resentment for a lesson, if a tenured professor gets vexed when a depressed French existentialist regrets to exist, if destiny's amidst, saying: "If life's a bitch then death's a sexist; making an exit if, there's any vestige of estrogen meddling with this incestuous message stenciled on her left tit. If that's an expletive, X-it; if it's impeditive to feminine excellence, then censors get a left breast to caress instead. I'm the best kept repentance. Every sentence invented in Venice is a penance; it all depends when your pen indents it. This is the cassette testament, ejected from decks, metrics flexed again on diskettes, a potentially eminent endeavor, kinetic gestures, sped indefinitely, adrenaline revving pleasant medleys, defending the tenets of Alfred Lord Tennyson; even though Kevin's descended from demented American peasant tenants in insect infested rented tenements, forgetting memorable glens, amending texts not intended for dispensing, instead of recommending them to appendix sections. Digressing, it's like letting Fin tend to picket fences, jettison to the hedges, hence, the edge of Miss Betsy's residence. He gets pensive when coquettish wenches, reminiscent of Bo Derrick in *10*, reference epic spaghetti western temptresses they envy, brunette tresses feathered and dresses drenched in a terrible Tempest, they wept to replenish, whether wedded or not tethered by leather to Teddies and Ed's weathering bed threats in the Serengeti trenches, I read, can discredit eleven dead gazette editors with twenty-six letters, in tenses like red men intending on treading to tents intensely, addressed to every prevalent Kennedy senator, sent in penicillin scented envelopes with an essential penciled in *Kevin* and a textured wren emblem to end this threaded genesis: The general consensus is this phonetic etiquette's credible evidence suggests it's ethically imperative you pessimists get the gist this second; discrepancies were remnants deftly meant to be pent in, like a flick in the locket, get it? I'm in-da-pendent. Conceptually clever; a ref you met recollecting to when the Met's win the pennant. My method's an Emmitt Smith reception. Medals and patents pending. I get irreverent, like epileptic reverends into edible experimental Bedouin medicines; my tendency to pen these repetitive measures, was never indebted to Escher's segmented ledges, unless your impressing I invested in his gem of a stretched Tetris dimension: it's setting incessantly convexes accredited forensic assessments by Mensa members with leverage; but this is no retrospective of his perspective perfection. This corrective lens is denser than getting perplexed, yet, genuflecting out of respect to complexity finessed in baguettes; regretfully, I'm senseless, a penniless tenor, cheddar cheese expended with unleavened bread to the Nth degree. I'll never be a success due to the wretchedness of brevity, but F-it, B, I'll forever be the breathless emcee, a legend you'll never see: the heavenly sent entity known to his friends as Kevin C!" Bes blessed me with cess to be hex free, no enemies, preferably, with 'Nessa next to me. It's chemistry; get ready to get gassed like dented Chevy's at Hess and Getty, headed directly to Connecticut to get a better connect for cut by the Hefty. Aesthetically, I definitely just presented a tempting semblance of tremendous pent in splendorous vignettes, yes, it's generatively strenuous but that's just the pen tip enlisted to stick these lecherous pricks with. Tension collects like sediments in cliffs; an endless reflection's abyss is detecting this subjective death kiss's objective. Accept it; except if your obsessive and discontent with a pathetic pet's ineptness; let me in: What's fresh about record executive discotheque receptions? Expecting percentages yet neglectful with your tax exemptions! An elephant never forgets, it's heavy, annexed by the temperance sects, so don't mess with Texas, or the detested president elect will set it in the next election, possessing the dreaded web's excessive tender to get it, yet again, selected to play chess with the census, they benefit when there's an epidemic spreading, letting extra Techs in, yet preventing a bevy of Mexican chefs from getting proper checks or acceptance; my veteran cadet friend embedded in Mecca said it best: "I'm ready to wet this oppressive Texan Methodist! I dreamt I pressed a licensed Smith-and-Wesson to the head of a Heston effigy and defected!" He mentioned his preference when the weapon clicks: "It's just protection!" Then I'm a pro-Tec contestant; my projectile's a lead protest lent to my nemesis's leprous flesh like a petty ten cents for emphasis, severed red, disconnecting appendages like pheasant necks, suppressing intensive extremity mending by medical attention;

asbestos infected abscesses fizz and fester like refreshing blended cherries and lemons in beverages, dispensing several venoms within endocrine systems, letting epinephrine injections enter, your energy's ebbing, empty intestines clenching like wrenches, compressed in septic engines, a rectum's feculent digested mess of excrement in your stench-ridden denim; retina extending death is present for the menaced, steadily fret, your treasured generic fleck of an essence is jetting, trekking effortless as a leopard to mesh by placenta with celestial sections; rest in the tepid depth as an exceptionally breathless specimen in tennis kicks, like Pegasus, cemented seminally till tendons rip. My revenge is quenched like electrolytes to sweat; so sweat it, for the distressed West Memphis six like seven consecutive dentist visits. Yes, I confessed terrorist vendettas I rendered to this metal bench I allegedly erected in jest, or was it in justice? In the event of God's silence this is ubiquitous substance.

Mister Kelly

Suppose/ I pose as a priest/ and dose a piece/of host for the feast/ with peyote and leak;/ rose to my feet like yeast,/ propose a toast to me/ old folks tweak/ they hold their rosaries/ closely/ like a lucky clover leaf/ their throats squeak:/ "Oh, Geez!/ We heard the holy/ ghost speak/ through gold teeth!"/ Toking weed,/ as I preach to provoke them;/ I give back like a polish thief./ The pope of the east/ coast moping on a sofa seat,/ alone my soul flees/ from me zoning in steeples asleep/ pupils peeping beneath/ my Oakley's/ my doting invokes Josephine/ as a ghost in a sheet;/ we eloped in Thebes,/ her broken ovaries/ opened like a lotus leaf/ breaching for the over breed/ Even though she's over me,/ Napoleon scolded me;/ I awoke with beads/ of sweat all over me;/ It was all a dream,/ or so it seamed,/

Supposedly…

I slowly heat/ 'dro it keeps/ me so relieved,/ knowing these/ sophistries/ can mold sheep to bleat/ so they won't bleed;/ I goad teens/ to leave B.O.C.E.S./ they won't need/ a bogus degree/ to grow weed/ and goatees/ like Cochez/ Hopefully/ They'll owe me/ an O.Z/ and some stolen O.C.'s;/ we loathe these/ fogies/ so we load these/ subs like hoagies-/ now they're poking up posies!/ Nose like an oboe blowing C-/ notes with coke fiends/ who don't ski/ but still see more snow then cold peaks/ in the Fo' Seas'/ Fo' sheez,/ they told me:/ "Yo, you roll cones with folds like canolis;/Yo, B,/ we're out for cheese like pirogis!"/ We were low key/ like a Nokia phone beat/ we sold keys/ and bought gold beams/ we were Co-D's:/ Closer than Boo-Boo to Yogi;/ Big L to O.C.;/ Gumby to Pokey;/ Butter to Whole wheat;/ Luke to Obie;/ T.S. to Brody;/ Legs to hosiery;/ Kid Rock to Joe C.,/

Supposedly…

I was so close to defeat/ sipping tea by Sobe/ I jokingly/ told police/ I groped my niece's/ mocha cheeks/ and secreted a load of seed/ over her Grover sheets./ Peed over her feet,/ while I played Jodeci;/ I gloated for weeks/ knowing she/ could keep a secret like Mona Lis',/ and wouldn't phone police,/ and lead them to this old home I lease,/ right by Jones Beach,/ keep it close to Queens,/ where I post for weeks/ and homeless freaks/ seen on posters are known to sleep/ if they bone my homies/ for no fee/ dome me/ and always know to eat/ protein,/ I coat teens,/ faces and hair like afro-sheen./ Your no queen,/ so choke on my choad sleaze,/ rolling on "E,"/ O.D.'ing, / hoes, I want to see/ your bows meet,/ your exposed knees,/ so roll up your capris,/ and imagine your posing/ on the cover of that Vogue 'zine./ Stress the seams/ of my Girbaud jeans/ like Crow's feet/ do to the place your face and dome meet,/ evoking emotion,/ as you proceed,/ to jerk me like Jamaicans do to goat meat,/

Supposedly…

Noah knows these/ oceans of flows can be/ so deep;/ each notions a sea,/ it's supposed to teem,/ with meaning, that boat in the stream,/ floating by steam,/ be the mode to reach/ my goal like a notable goalie's cleats;/ so I don't need/ Dover Beach/ to know this whole globe is poetry,/ even toads in moats croak notes in Troches,/ even those who don't read/ O.E./ know to quote me/ even though their dopey/ like my old neighbor Joe D./ on Codeine/ and won't heed/ how a trope is mostly,/ a Xenophobes ode to a road he/ probably won't see./ So I'm Edgar Allen, Po' ringing groceries,/ woe is me, / flow uncontrollably,/ focus to keep/ the prose clean,/ spoke degrees,/ wrote the heat,/ but won't be seen,/ on TV screens,/ the way it's supposed to be,/

Supposedly….

There's no peace/ overseas,/ the future is so bleak,/ the overseers/ are scoping these/ robed sober sheiks,/ cloaked in deceit,/ oh, we're so discrete,/ roaming their streets,/ holding pieces,/ boldly/ like the Trojan Fleet/ on ponies;/ reaping Roman peeps,/ swords won't sheathe,/ while seeking the Golden Fleece./ Word is born breached,/ why won't we,/ impeach this phony/ and teach his cronies,/ there's no ole' oak tree,/ so we must be/ tying the golden rope round the office soda machine,/ it's baloney,/ I'm still loathing/ Kathy Lee and Cody,/ while the souls of Cambodian homies/ goes into clothing/

Supposedly.

Ten O'clock Jokes

I sin against
God,
with this
dialog
I'm speaking,
while eating
hog's
feet in
the synagogue
on the weekend.

I got nobody
to lie to,
like the Cyclops in the
cave;
trying to see you
through these bars
but this spoon's con-
cave.

They tried to starve me
in the hole, so
I ate some moss
dried out;
then opened up my mouth
to let the moths
fly out;
they circled my head
like a halo,
as I fell dead
I said:
"Tell the orderlies in the unit
it's safe to sell my meds!"

I haven't been right for
seventeen years,
since my first therapist said:
"Kevin needs peers."

This is my life on an easel,
every brush with death's
liable to lead to
a recital
with the needle;
so faded
I'm see through.

Follow the leader
and bleed a liter
with me, B,
keep receiving these
evil demons,
screaming
through speakers,
deceiving me,
like:

"God wants you dead,
in the sod instead
of breathing;
the body of Poseidon
lying headless
in the Garden of Eden!"
If your starving we're eating,
two heathens,
like Eve and
Adam, leaving,
if biting an
apple means
cleaving an
atom. See
what can happen

when I proceed to get
at 'em? I even

got more peeps
then those Easter treats;
I once dosed a piece
and saw Jesus creep.
I need the cheeb'
it gives relief and release;
keep it in a box to
collect the kef,
just in case my next
paycheck is weak.

The young Nietzsche,
leak in his lungs,
speaking in tongues
in cheek,
tucking a piece un-
derneath
his beat up
Enyce.

I feel like I and I alone,
created the Earth with cyclones,
to quake craters and dirt;
I waited at first,
lurked in outer space,
awaked,
then invaded the Earth;
I made the birds,
take turns,
taking turds
on your face;
you're late to work,
and your perc-
olator spurts
coffee on your new shirt.

I do dirt,
and if I come to understand that your planning
to murder me,
I'll most certainly, turn your Clarks from tan in-
to burgundy!

I don't pop
a smirk,
unless I'm popping
a perk,
dropping
a verse, perfectly,
rocking a turban
on top,
like Papa Smurf,
serving a flock of his Turks;
I got an aversion to cops,
they circle the spot
yearning to stop
a perp
they watch
working the block
with some herb in his sock;
pocket got a wad of dirt,
turning a profit
cause Papa got to cop
his bird a Prada skirt.
Earth got to look proper if
she gets spotted
and served,
if they really got the nerve,
me and my bird
can shock the world.

I became the God of words,
serving Herbs in Birkenstocks,
who think they're punk rockers,
but their moms is doctors,
and their pops work in stocks;
while mine worked on the docks.
I'm a burner cocked,
learning to pop,
like a virgin on top,

cock
my monocle
to ogle
the blocks
optical Popsicles
properly abolish
all possibly
hostile obstacles
from Hollis, Queens
to the hottest
tropical spots,

I bring drama

like I'm Sophocles,
rocking soccer cleats,
knock you to the ground and stomp
you till your Esophagus bleeds;
lock you in a sarcophagus,
but forgot the keys.
I get possessive with my essence
like apostrophe *S's*;
I taught Apostles these lessons,
in this Apocryphal section.

A powerful text,
reflect on
as I get slept on,

like a Seally Posturpedic
with the pillow
you wept on;

I'm Teflon,
so no amount of
shit is sticking.
Quit your bitching,
so what if Kevin
came into your kitchen
and kicked the keg in;
then lifted up his dick and
told your chick
to lick the webbing.
Chicks complain
my knob
spews globs
too thick;
come to the crib
to give me brain
in ski gog-
gles and a lobster bib;
Alot of these rappers wish
they were a mobster's kid,
but that's imposter,
like whites with dreads
rocking Rasta knits.

I'm a mad
Mick cynic
with a pad
to script in,
fit my dad's
description,
when I'm in my lab
sipping nips,
getting pickled a bit,
nitwits quick

to pick up a picket,
and sticker hip
hop's hits
explicit.
I could give a big hip-
po shit if,
your little kids

listen,

flick their Bics, Zip-
pos and Crickets,
to this spliff,
hit it,
and get lifted
without the cliff
or lift ticket;
get livid.
I'll divvy up the profits,
I came equipped
with props,
so tell the grips to quit;
I'll rip the script,
like an actor getting pissed.
Splitting zips
into nickels to pitch,
flip them to little kids,
kibbles and bits for pups,
Fisticuffs,
uh-uh,
we lift them up,
with nick-
el plated fifths
and pumps,
Hem them up,
stitch them with
thimbles to thumbs,

able to

crumble these crumbs,
humbled they hum,
the songs I sung.

I don't give a fuck
like a celibate nun,
to hell with the funds,
I rhyme for the intelligent ones;
your words are like nines,
mine's
an Elephant gun.
So open up your mouth
and let your skeleton run.

I kiss my crucifix,
then I start to brood a bit,
like a rutabaga,
getting to the root of it,

I used to

bum cigarettes
when I couldn't make due;
shit...
with a can of tuna
and a brew
I could make stew;

I used to

wake
up at eight,
and bake
an eighth
of shake,
straight

to my face,
but why waste?
I delay fate
and save
a taste
so I can get blazed
on a later date.
Cake
is at stake,
and I can't afford to make

a mistake,

I'm a true disgrace,
sitting in a burnt out
tenement next
to a wall
with glue on my face;
holding a paper bag
(I hate my dad!)
That's why the only friend
I've made
is this razor blade.
The end is near,
fuck that, the end
is nigh! and
I'm a end
it now,
when I'm F-ing high!

I got an '82 Olds
and the trunk screams;
there's no subwoofer,
it's full of drunk teens!
I take seven
fans from Weezer,
and make them Kevin
Skeezers;

all that it takes is seven-
teen Tequizas!
I must be god,
'cause in bed they scream:
"Jesus!"
Plus these,
preteens
seam to be
squeamish;
green,
like they've never seen
semen before.

Drop your
Lees to the floor
then you're
leaving a whore.

Eating a slice of pizza,
in boxers and a wife beater,
my life's theater,

drama,

I might flee from,
Fee-
    Fi-
        Foe's come,
three;
    four;
        five guns,
he might score some,
or
he might take it!

Duct tape
the baked kids,
For fuck sake

they're shaking!
Rake in
their bacon,
now we're taking
a vacation,
amongst the Haitians.

My neighbor's making,
a fake tooth out
of a peg in my basement,
placed it
in and grinned like a ham
without the eggs and the bacon.

I'm the type to think
about death on a regular basis;
I've seen heads razor'd up,
left with irregular faces.
K's a Daigo
raiding bodegas
for Flav-A-
Ice and Garcia Vegas;
blazing papers
containing the name
of our savior
till the day the
Martians invade us.

Now I lay
in the place
the Raiders play
with Lady J;
dedication is pressing
your own records
with a razor blade.
I want the same
radio play
as Hova,

so

when I'm gray
and older,
maybe sober,
I can buy an acre in Maine
and then pave it over

so

I can do do-
nuts in my new range rover!

Cashier
slash
rapper,
slash
porno film actor,
shit!
Now half my
faggot fans
cop my film after
this!

Listen,

this is just a description,
of my life
on the mission,
no ice
on my wrist,
just mice
in the kitchen.

Listen, the

Gestapo pops
an optimistic

Mick,
heater hot,
fist
got blisters
dropped the biscuit,
like he forgot
the oven mitts;
loving Glover flicks,
Mel's role was compatible,
with or with-
out the capital,
spat a jewel,
let it cool to coal;
blaze a Kool or two,
then I'm good to

go.

These Baptist rappers
are vaginal activists,
acting irrational,
scratching their rashes,
in the back of my class,
passing the Masengill;
it's a fact I'm saccharin,
I'm lacking in tact,
they lacking in skill!

Back to laughing
at Catholics,
crack back a Labatt,
or perhaps a Pabst

and listen,

as I attack
the Vatican,
for acting

Christian,
slap them
with phylactery straps and
an Act of Contrition;

they had to listen,

as I asked them,
to take back my baptism,
and turn me back into a bastard.

I rap fast till my asthma hits,
then flip it backwards
like Nas on track six;
ask the bricks,
who's a star like asterisks,
with tactics,
like Cactus Jack in
matches.

A Cat that'll
slap
you to the mat, till
tacks stick
to your back.

A catastrophe leads,
to you being a casket's seed,
gradually
hatching into a tree.
You can't hack it,
like a lumberjack with
a bad back
and no axe
to cleave.
You can't ask
to leave,
it's such a tragedy,

perhaps if we
weep we
can see a leaf;
there's no need in belief-
just look at the fruit you eat!

Nietzsche
never tried to speak
with me,
Judas
wouldn't eat
with me;
what's beef?
I told Hindi's
not to feast on it.
I gave you Easter bonnets
to rock when you meet
the Pontiff.
I sonically speak sonnets,
through an emcee
on leak and chronic.

I'm nice with these,
so please,
pass the mic like a
pipe for peace,
mind your *p's*
and *q's* as I
spoon you these
rice and peas.

It's time to sleep

and when your eyes close,
I'm already there;
in your dreams rockin'
the same sweater
Freddy wears.

I can turn a grown ass man
into a little bitch
hugging
a teddy bear.

You can talk about
your block,
and how you
keep it real
there;
I'm a shoot you with
my glock,
so you can
keep a wheel
chair!

I'm everywhere;
I'm the mist in the air,
beware!
This
is not a dis,
I'm not pissed,
but it's
impossible
not to notice him,
since
my skin tones
got me demoted
to his clone
or opponent in
this rap race
lacks taste
like a rat racing
to lick
the lactating
tit of a blonde bitch
in black face,

face it

class is closed,
for the son of a
motherless goat;
the coven coated
me in blood inside
a hovering boat;
frozen,
smothered,
hoping my throat
will open,

but,

I'm underground,
and your just adjacent
to the basement, B.
I get pleasure from
shooting you,
so I always aim to please.

I'd rather see
the cadaver of (censored)
gradually
gathering maggots
in the back of a Cadillac,
holding a candelabra,
abracadabra,
there you have it,
sans the rabbits
and hats, it's magic,
thanking a crank addict
for this murderous act,
but,
vic'in this nit-wit-
Caesar-
having faggot with

the Dragon isn't
tragic.
You couldn't imagine
matching wits
with the Catholic;
I'm simply ravishing,
his majesty,
I have an entire parish in
back of me.
Even crews
of Jews
who stay strapped with
phylacteries.

I easily,
eat an emcee,
eagerly;
I'm an elitist-
collegiate emcee.
Call me mercury,
'cause I keep track of degrees.
While you work
the chocolate factories
getting fudge packed.
You're the only thug that
rocks a Von Dutch hat-

fuck that!

I'll buck back;
bluh-
blap!!
Oh snap!
Rat-a-
tat-tat!!
A Blood bath!
"Blah-blah-
bombs..."

Shah's say:
"Blah-blazhay-
blah-cadavers-
Allah-Allah-
Akbar
blah-pah'k-da
cah's-tah-
Walla-Walla!"

Pardon me Pah-
tna!
But
that's what
I call a
tapped
cells chatter.

I must confess, love,
I'm messed up;
when I get
sessed up,
your wet blood's
reminiscent of ketchup
or Pez
dispensed from the neck up.

What's the sense in a check up?

Irony's riding shotgun
in the back seat
of the V;
'cause Irony's got a shotgun
cocked back
in the back seat
of the V.

Matter of fact,
I saw duke's ad in

the back of that magazine;
he had a faggot's lean,
showin' his tats,
trying to act mean;
airbrushed the acne,
combing his hair
like a drag queen.
Perhaps he,
inspires me

to write a book
and pitch it to Oprah;
it's called:
How to Get Your Bitch Off of the Sofa

Brought over dope
in hopes
I'd rope her.
That bitch overdosed,
got coke on both us.

Your gear's busted,
the only time you feel fly's
when your dusted,
bugging on the rooftop
flapping your arms;
your Aunt's
at your wake,
rapping you psalms,
grabbing your palms,
smacking the asphalt,
cat's cracking:
"What an asshole!
He could have lasted
and been the next Flava
from Nassau!"
But instead your dead,
headless,

and what's left is
reminiscent of lettuces;
family and friends,
in debt,
not enough cheddar
for your funeral expenses.
So when they check
the census
it's like you still existed.

What A&R in his right mind
would want to market you;
when your grill's busted,
like there's no barbeque?
All you do is chain smoke
and think about dying;
write a rhyme and
kill yourself,
while the ink's drying.

I really fucking hate you!
How can I make it clearer?
Look you right in the eye,
and put my fist through the mirror.

Subliminal flickers,
project
criminal pictures,
with afflictions
like Gary Glitter,
tickling kids.

Did I stutter?
Uh-uh.
Boxcutter
blade under
the tongue
run through

skin like butter;
Every other
word I utter
is utterly gutter.
You just a
pup stuck
under
your mother's
udders
with your baby brothers
suckling; sucker
punk-mother-
fucker suffer,
when the shudder clicks,
like snuff flicks,
funded with
government

money,

It's the big dog
muzzled
in court your mug
looking like a jigsaw
puzzle;
I've been saw trouble,
that day in the park,
prayed you wouldn't start
shit,
you
did
and I slit
you;
twin buck fifties make
you
grin like Pac-
man.
I still can't understand

how you got your chin back,
man!

That fat chick
you
screwing got eyes
like Bernie Mac's,
man!
Nose like Patrick Ewing
and shoe size
like Shaq's,
man!
They call her "Oboe"
'cause her nose blows
C-notes;
yo, tell Oboe to call me
she owes me for coke!
She sleeps
around and needs
a deep
V.D. inspection;
she's a fiend
who stole
your whole
D-
VD collection!
She brags about how she's
seen Eazy-
E's erection;
and shows off the scars
from her three
C-sections!
So many yeast infections,
bitch should have a bake sale.
Maybe then her three
seeds could even make bail!

The only time I wear

a suit's
to beat a case in court;
or at a funeral,
to see the face of a corpse.
So in case you thought,
K ain't raw,
chill...
like an artist
in Antarctica,
just wait until
the paint thaws.
Then,

get shot
in your back's hump;
now your name
rings bells
like Quasimodo
dwellin' in steeples.
You can't see me
like Vern in Earnest
sequels;
the only time I keep
it gully's when
I'm burning herb with
seagulls;
so tell your peoples,
to digest my text
and turn my words to fecal.

My hell is deep,
this quill quells all;
a salt in the welt,
is worth three on the scald.

When my Earth calls,
all work stalls;
no more offin'

these Herbs soft
as foam Nerf balls.

I'm heated but calm,
reading a psalm;
holy like
Jesus' palms,
holding a
fetus embalmed.

I see through souls
like air bubbles
on a Nike;
when I rap people like:
"There's trouble
on the mic!"
Packing duffle
bags on the pike;
while you pull bananas
out your muffler's
pipe.
You must've been
hyped,
encouraged too much in
your life;
I'm a punch
you right,
upside your head like
my mail order Russian wife,
Sike!
Flustered
like,
"I must've been lunchin'
type-
dusted
to write this bugged shit!"
never trust the government,
or the one I'm with,

I'm numb to this;
the hustle got me buzzin'
feeling like a bumble bee's cousin,

looking down

at your corpse
like it doesn't
need pants;
chop it up
and use the pieces
to fertilize a dozen
weed plants.

Looking back,

I lend a gram
of coke to my man,
so he can sniff it
in
the shape of a pentagram;
he's sentimental, man,
an
ex-heavy metal fan.

We got 24,
like Keifer Sutherland,
to get plenty more
of this reefer smuggled in.
These fiends bugging,
making my beeper buzz again,
but it's
the K
to the E-vin;
I stay
even
from the day
to the evening.

I've seen snow,
but I've never
been skiing.
My burners a pooch
from the precinct.
I'm Turner; he's Hooch-
retrieving.
When I shoot he drools
like he's eating,
and Dude, he do
snap,
the bullets are Scooby-doo
snacks,
so Dude, I wouldn't do
that.
He's my dog,
you're just Scrappy
with that puppy power;
you're a New York Minute,
I'm a Boston Hour.
I rep New England
like that cup of chowder,

I'd rather it rain, but I'd love a shower.

It's the man
who killed God
when he spoke his
name,
wild like jokers
in a poker
game
he's supposed to
reign
but he's opposed to
fame.

He needs a dame,
but he's not the type
of guy to settle down
in a marriage;
if his baby cried
he'd blow weed smoke
in the carriage;
and how the fuck
would he manage,
to give your finger
karats
without a rabbit
attached to it?
You see this smoke linger-
he's more then just an
addict.
The last habit
he kicked left a nun
in traction;
when he rolls blunts
he throws a ton
of hash in;
he's packing,
a gun
for fun and fashion.

I'm missing
my twin in
prison
and I'm wishing
I could visit him,
sit with him,
and hit him
off with a bit of izm;
picture it, him
and his miz's
twisting a griz
of shit up in a blizzy.

They have an epiphany,
figured
out the big mystery:
"If we could script history,
differently,
we'd switch positions
with Mister T;
just to pity thee.
Live in Italy,
specifically,
Sicily,
twisting trees
in Swisher Sweets,
hitting that bitch Tiffany!"

I think we're alone now.

Is it O.K. to be low brow?
She said she don't swallow,
I said:
"Relax and try it;
my semen's covered on
the Atkin's diet."
She said:
"How was that?"
I tried to act excited,
rolled over and
went to sleep:
"It's time to practice silence..."

Fuck a microphone,
I got more bars
then a xylophone,
I write a tighter poem,
when I'm high at home,
I want to be like Mike,
Corleone;

when I die alone.

It used to be,
you choose
Dudes
who knew you
to read your eulogy
Dudes
who knew you
juiced bluish swooshes
exclusively
like news sweeps;
Dudes
who know the truth is,

I'm too ruthless;
I'm a boot you
and leave you toothless.
Duke,
I'm a shoot you like those
two mooks
in the movies
Menace and *Juice*.
Get used to abuse,
you're cruising
for a bruising
and a contusion or two;
make no confusion
I'm using a pseudonym to
elude police,
and allude to using
a 'lude or two to release,
the beast
and tune my attitude
to Buddhist beliefs.
Dude,
I suggest
you get

a new address;
if you too
moody to invest
in this rap shit
you should move
to Budapest.
Who's the best?
I don't know, but I can guess
who is fresh;
you, in a blender, flesh
shredded to confetti,
steadily.
Blades remi-
niscent of Pesci
holding two machetes.
Dude,

you're in no position
to tell me shit;
dressed like a referee,
trying to sell me kicks:
"Kevin,
here's an eleven,
I think you got room."
Nah, a size
twelve will fit,
run back to the stock room.

Life is a test,
at death, you get
graded.
I'd hate to sound jaded,
but there's more at stake
then potential invasions,
attacking Iraq's
a way to make
cake for vacations;
Asia ain't

complacent,
they really hate us.
They keep their missiles
placed adjacent
to our military's bases.
and weapon
inspectors neglect
to check
every peasant's
residence,

Sike!

Imagine me picking
sides
in a fight;
I'm illin'
like
Ryan White.

That kid's still
dying, right?

In the mean time,
while the rest
heckle Mecca
I'll be
shackled like
Ali.
In prison
I'll read.
Treating my cell
like a tabernacle.
Who bit the Apple?
Were we Babel
with our towers proud?
Questions spoke aloud;
I check the time:

the hours now.
Surely there's truth
in my certain sound;

I'll bring drama

like Thebes until
my curtain's down.
I put the hurting down,
punch lines
with brass knuckles,
harass nuckas,
acting like your crass uncle,
sippin' brass monkey,
the fourth Beastie-
on your porch with a tree
full of the leaky,

I breathe deeply!